The text of this book is a much–shortened
version of the Grimm fairytale
translated by Margaret Hunt.

Also illustrated by Adrie Hospes
THE MAGIC HORSE

Library of Congress Cataloging in Publication Data
Main entry under title:

The six swans.

   SUMMARY: A retelling of how the King's
daughter rescues her six brothers from the
enchantment imposed on them by their wicked
stepmother.
   "The text of this book is a much-shortened
version of the Grimm fairytale translated by
Margaret Hunt"
   (1. Fairy tales. 2. Folklore-Germany)
I. Grimm, Jakob Ludwig Karl, 1785-1863.
Die sechs Schwäne. II. Hunt, Margaret Raine,
1831-1912, tr. III. Hospes, Adrie, illus.
PZ8.S365   398.2'1'0943   74-8580
ISBN 0-07-030475-0
ISBN 0-07-030476-9 (lib. bdg.)

Printed in Holland for McGraw-Hill Book Company.
First published in Holland under the title of
DE ZES ZWANEN 1973.
First published in Great Britain by the Bodley Head Ltd.

First distribution in the United States of America by
McGraw-Hill Book Company.

THE BROTHERS GRIMM
The Six Swans

Illustrated by ADRIE HOSPES

McGraw-Hill Book Company
New York   St. Louis   San Francisco

Once upon a time as a certain King was out hunting in a great forest, he lost his way. Through the trees he saw an old woman coming towards him. She was a witch. "Good woman," he said, "will you show me the way through the forest?"

"Yes, Lord King," she answered, "that I will, but on one condition. I have a daughter and if you will make her your queen, I will show you the way."

The King consented. Although the girl was very beautiful she did not please him and he could not look at her without secret horror. But he took her up on his horse, and the old woman showed him the way out of the forest.

The King had already been married once, and had by his first wife seven children, six boys and a girl, whom he loved more than anything else in the world. But he now feared that his new wife might not treat the children well, so he took them away to a lonely castle. It was so surrounded by trees that he himself would not have found it, if a wise woman had not given him a magic ball of yarn. When he threw the ball down before him, it unrolled itself and showed him the way.

The King went so frequently to see his dear children that the Queen was curious and wanted to know where he went. So she gave money to his servants, and they betrayed the secret to her.

The Queen had learned the art of witchcraft from her mother and now she made six shirts of white silk for the King's sons and inside each one she sewed a charm.

She took the shirts and followed where the ball of yarn led her. The children saw from a distance that someone was approaching and thinking that it was their dear father, full of joy they ran to meet him.

The Queen then threw
the shirts over the boys,
and no sooner had the silk
touched their bodies
than the children were
changed into swans,
and flew away. The
Queen went home delighted,
thinking she had got rid
of her step-children,
but the girl had remained
in the castle, and the
Queen knew nothing about her.

Next day when the King went to visit his children he found only his daughter. She told him what she had seen from the castle window; how her brothers had flown away in the shape of swans. The King mourned but he could not believe that the Queen could have done this wicked deed.

Meanwhile the poor girl thought, "I cannot stay here alone. I must go and look for my brothers," and when night came, she ran away and went straight into the forest. She walked all that night, and the following day also until she could go no farther for weariness. Then she saw a forest hut, and in it she found a room with six little beds. She crept under one to hide and lay down on the hard floor.

Just before sunset the girl heard a great rustling, and six swans
came flying into the hut. Alighting on the ground
they hissed at each other, blowing their feathers
in all directions.

Then the maiden saw they were her brothers. The boys were no less

delighted to see their little sister but their joy was short-lived.

They said to her, "Only for one quarter-of-an-hour each evening can we lay aside our feathers and regain our human form. After that we become swans again."

Their sister wept and said, "Can no one set you free of this magic?" They answered, "Only you can set us free. For six years you must neither speak nor laugh, and in that time you must sew together six shirts of starwort for us. And if one single word falls from your lips, all your work will be lost."

And when the brothers had said this the quarter-of-an-hour was over.

Then their sister went out and gathered starwort and began to sew. All day she sat at her work and at night she would climb into a tree to rest.

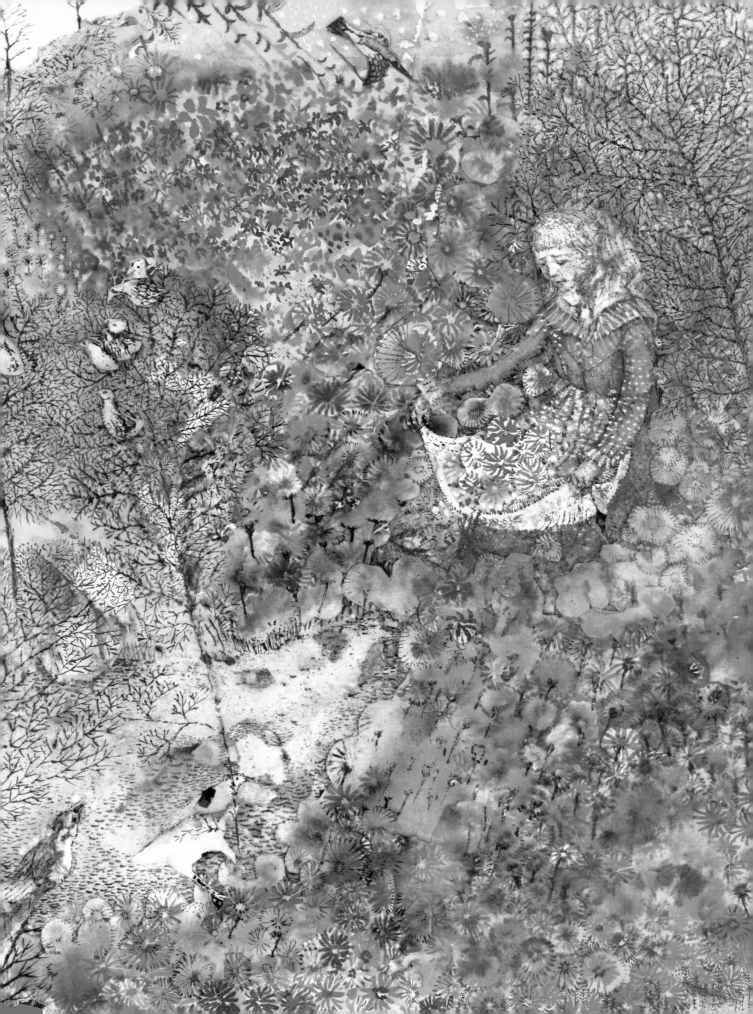

Early one morning a young King with his huntsmen passed under the tree in which the girl was resting. They called to her to come down but she made no answer. As they questioned her further she threw down her golden necklace hoping they would go away, for she could speak no word to them, and soon she had given them everything but her shift. The huntsmen, however, did not let themselves be turned aside, but climbed the tree and fetched her down.

The huntsmen led the girl before the King. The King asked, "Who are you and what are you doing in that tree?" But she did not answer. He put the question in every language he knew, but she remained as mute as a fish. As she was so beautiful, the King's heart was touched. He put his mantle on her, put her before him on his horse, and carried her to his castle. He placed her by his side at table, and her modest bearing pleased him so much that he said, "She is the one whom I wish to marry, and no other woman in the world."

The King, however, had a wicked mother who did not like this marriage. "Who knows," said she, "from whence comes the creature who cannot speak? She is not worthy of a King!" But the King married the beautiful girl.

After a year had passed, the young Queen brought her first child into the world, and the old woman took the baby away from her and hid it, smearing the Queen's mouth with blood as she slept. Then the old woman went to the King and accused the Queen of having eaten the child. The King would not believe it, and would not allow anyone to do his wife injury. The young Queen, however, sat continually sewing the shirts, and cared for nothing else.

Some time later when she again bore a beautiful boy, the wicked old woman used the same treachery, but still the King would not believe ill of his wife.

But when the old woman stole away a newly-born child for a third time, and accused the Queen, who did not utter one word of defense, the King could do no other than deliver her over to justice. She was sentenced to death by fire.

People assembled in the square. It was
the last day of the six years during
which the girl was not to speak or
laugh. The six shirts were ready, only
the left sleeve of the sixth was wanting,
and she held them over her arm. Just as
the fire was lit she saw the six swans
flying through the air, and her heart
leapt with joy. As the swans flew down
she threw the shirts over them.

As the shirts touched them their feathers fell away and her brothers stood before her, vigorous and handsome. The youngest only lacked his left arm, and had in place of it a swan's wing. The Queen was saved from the fire. And now at last she could tell the King of the treachery of the old woman who had taken away her three children. Then to the great joy of the King and Queen the children were brought to the palace.

The King and the Queen with their three children and the Queen's six brothers lived for many years in happiness and peace.